D1308722

# Acknowledgements

This book would not have been written without the support and encouragement of Charudutt Mishra. And it wouldn't have survived without the editorial skills of Rohan Arthur. They have contributed as much to its final form as I have. Sangeetha Trivedi motivated me to rethink and rewrite most of the text. This, I think was the turning point in the genesis of the story. Maya Ramaswamy provided the much-needed artistic touch and has brought the book to life. In that sense, she has actually done the better half of the book. Aparajita Datta, herself a good writer also helped with editing and streamlining of the text. Without the support and hospitality of 'Sushil' (our real Dorje!), Tanzin Thinley and other enthusiastic members of the Youth Council of Kibber village, it would have been impossible to conceive this story. I thank Yash Veer Bhatnagar for useful suggestions and for his critical eye which helped improve the illustrations. Pavithra Sankaran nourished the book in its final stages and helped with design and production. Charu-Aparajita and Yash Veer-Krishna provided a home away from home during my stay at Mysore. I am indebted to the Whitley Fund for Nature for their support.

*Pranav*

Pranav's story opened a world I visited for the first time in life. But I couldn't have visited this wonderful world of the snow leopard had I not met Sushil and Lama in Charudutt's house. An intense session with Charudutt over the first reference images transported me to Spiti, and brought every image vividly to life. Invaluable critical evaluation by Yash Veer and Charudutt contributed immensely to the paintings. Thanks are also due to all at the Nature Conservation Foundation, especially Aparajita and Charudutt for making me feel totally at home in Mysore.

*Maya*

# Contents

The Ghost of the Snow     1

Nono: the Little King     7

In Search of Nono     12

The First Meeting     17

Belling the Cat!     23

On Nono's Trail     30

The Hidden Danger     33

The Hunt     40

The New Camp     46

The First Lessons     49

The Last Journey     53

Afterword: Return of the Snow Leopard     56

Glossary     60

# The Ghost of the Snow

Hari stands atop a cliff overlooking the deep gorges and vast meadows, scanning every rock and patch—for the ghost of the snow. At his side, Dorje, with craggy, practiced eyes, is searching too. The breeze is steady, nagging, cold.

There are no trees here. Bushy, cushion-like plants dot the undulating meadows and slopes. Towering snow-capped peaks touch the sky. Precipitous cliffs keep away all but the bravest. The blue sky is without a speck of cloud. We are in the Spiti Valley, high up in the Himalaya, home of the snow leopard—the ghost of the snow. Spring is a welcome change from the harshness of winter. Everywhere, the ruddy flowers of the season have begun to colour the rugged terrain. Farmers have begun to till their fields. Life has come full cycle in Spiti, to begin again.

For Hari and Dorje too, work has just started. As wildlife biologists, they are ruled by the seasons just like the animals they study. "It is a challenging life," thinks Hari to himself as he stretches a small cramp from his calf, "but what better place could I have chosen for my work than these dauntingly beautiful mountains?"

They have been camping at this spot for a week now. Hari's **altimeter** reads 4,200 metres. They are following the movements of a snow leopard that they had **radio-collared**, but it has been ten days since they last picked up a signal. Their first radio-collared snow leopard is missing. There is only one question in their minds: "Where is Dolma?"

In their search, Hari and Dorje left the camp and moved higher up - towards the cliffs and gorges. "Don't wait for us to have lunch, we may be late," Dorje called out to Tashi, their cook and camp attendant.

As they moved up the slope, Dorje took one of their regular trails holding the antenna in one hand, his other hand moving over the receiver control box. With headphones on, he listened for a signal each time they stopped. Hari went ahead looking for tracks on the patches of snow. The trail was steep and after

about two kilometres, took a sharp turn towards the gorge. Hari turned around and found Dorje waving frantically.

At this altitude, the air is thin, every breath is a struggle, and it is almost impossible to run, and yet, Hari was by Dorje's side in a flash. "I can hear a signal, sir!" said Dorje. Hari listened. The beeps were loud and clear. "She must be near and active," whispered Hari. The radio-collar around the snow leopard's neck was an 'activity collar' and the speed of the signals indicated whether she was moving or resting. You had to be within a certain distance for the antenna to pick up signals from the radio-collar, and the closer you were the stronger the beeps.

The quest had begun; it was now a question of time and patience before they could locate her. There was a cliff nearby and some rugged peaks in between the meadows. "A likely hiding place," thought Hari. He asked Dorje to look carefully on the cliffs. Dorje nodded and took the lead. Hari followed. They scanned the area, turning the antenna in each direction and trying hard to figure out where the signal was strongest.

Meandering through the thorny **Caragana** bushes, Dorje's sharp eye soon spotted a fresh footprint on a patch of snow. The tracks were accompanied by marks of a thick and long tail. "She has just been here," Dorje whispered. Experience told him that she would not have gone far. The two men followed the **pugmarks** cautiously for the next half-hour. Suddenly, Dorje froze. Hari slowed down and came inching towards him. Dorje pointed at a big boulder at the edge of the cliff, softly whispering - "Look there." Hari could see nothing. He looked again and his eye caught a small movement. It was Dolma, her radio-collar visible even from this distance. She was looking straight at them, and she appeared nervous. She had probably been there for some time, but spotting snow leopards is very difficult. They merge completely with their surroundings and only a movement betrays their presence. Hari and Dorje were relieved to find Dolma was unharmed.

As he watched the leopard Hari wondered to himself, "Could it be that Dolma is pregnant?" Almost as if reading his mind, Dorje said aloud, "Sir, I think she is going to have cubs." "It is possible," said Hari, "otherwise she would not have been missing for so long. And now she's not even moving." This was the first time in two years they had found her at this spot, and it was a rather odd place for her to be. Hari was intrigued, but it was getting late, and they decided to call it a day.

They returned to camp and broke the news of Dolma's reappearance to Tashi. The moon was full, and they celebrated the occasion over a cup of hot tea sitting around the fire. The next morning, the camp was buzzing with an energetic anticipation. They continued to receive a signal from the same site but they could not spot Dolma. While Hari decided to stay back at the camp with Tashi, Dorje decided to get two more men to help him track the elusive animal.

Dorje was from Kibber village in Spiti, where he lived with his wife and two daughters. He was a small, thin man, in his early thirties, who loved the mountains and its wildlife with the same passion that he had for Hindi films and cricket. His skills in tracking wildlife were unparalleled, always impressing the tourists he took on treks. When Hari, a wildlife biologist from Delhi, arrived here to study snow leopards for his PhD degree, Dorje found his life transformed with a new-found purpose.

The snow leopard is an animal that guards its secrets well. We know very little of its behaviour and what it needs to survive. Hari was interested in changing that, by finding out more about this enigmatic animal through his research. However, his interests went far beyond his study. He wanted to find ways to protect this beautiful species and what remained of its habitat, because he knew full well how endangered the snow leopard was. People hunt it for its thick, mottled coat and bones, and also kill its **prey** for meat. If nothing was done soon, the snow leopard would soon go extinct from the earth. Hari knew this and it was the reason he was here in the cold barren mountains of Spiti.

Hari was tall and lanky, with a quick smile and always ready for a chat with everyone in the village. This had made him a great favourite especially with the children who loved the interesting stories he told about animals. When Hari first came to the village, he sought an experienced hand to help him with his work, and Dorje was the natural choice. In their time together, Dorje had taught Hari more about the mountain and its ways than all his years of education could possibly have done. He had hired Dorje as his field assistant, but they were now fast friends. They worked side by side, and had come to love the snow leopards they were studying. And now, their Dolma was about to have cubs. They tracked her with renewed anxiousness.

# Nono: the Little King

Dolma had given birth to three cubs. After days of fruitless searching, Sherpa, one of the men from Kee village that Dorje had brought along to help track Dolma, had made the discovery. He had stumbled upon a cave one day, and found several pugmarks all around it. Wisely, he decided to bide his time until it was safe to enter the cave and search it. He told Tashi about it and they waited for the right opportunity. Soon, their patience was rewarded. One day they saw Dolma leave the cave. Containing their excitement until she was a safe distance away, they entered, armed with a torch and a long stick. From one dark corner, they heard soft, insistent mewing. Their torch beam revealed three beautiful snow leopard cubs huddled in a corner. They looked up with wide open eyes only to retreat and stay calm in a corner. They could not have been more than a month old.

Two days later, while tracking Dolma, Dorje came across a bharal kill a few hundred yards from the camp in a ravine. Bharal or Blue Sheep are wild relatives of goat and sheep. "Must be Dolma's doing," Dorje said to himself as he examined the **carcass**. It was a big male with large horns. As they behave a little like goats and a little like sheep, the bharal are given a unique scientific name – *Pseudois*, meaning false sheep. Snow leopards hunt them for food.

It was clear that Dolma and her cubs intended to stay in the cave for some time. Hari's team found a few more kills made by her. They requested people from the village to avoid going towards the cave.

Hari moved to Pin Valley after a few months. This was a smaller valley nearby where he wanted to radio-collar two more snow leopards. Sherpa, who had worked with them for a few months, accompanied Hari. Dorje stayed at the camp with Tashi and kept an eye on the cave and spent a lot of time watching herds of bharal. The lambs had already been born; their gamboling and antics brought the pastures to life.

One sunny morning Dorje was in a cheerful mood, humming a song on his routine trek up to the cave. Just as he neared it, a shape emerged from within

the dark interiors into the beam of sunlight. It had a golden glow. "Dolma!" Before Dorje could believe his eyes, Dolma emerged followed by the three cubs. She walked slowly and sat down near the entrance. One of the cubs was rubbing her head against her mother and one was playing with Dolma's tail. The third cub was a male with a much larger head and sat looking over the rocks much like a little king surveying his kingdom. "Nono," Dorje said to himself, "he should be called Nono – the king."

There was something about Nono that fascinated Dorje. He noticed that his tail was twisted at the tip, unlike the other two cubs. Hari had taught him to look for such signs to identify individual animals. As Dorje watched Nono, he also noticed a small split in the right ear. He noted these features in his field diary carefully.

As time passed the cubs grew in size and strength. Often Dolma and the three cubs would spend hours sunning themselves near the cave. About one year after they were born, Dorje saw the three cubs accompany their mother on hunts. They did not yet participate in the hunts, but stayed nearby to watch and learn from Dolma. Dorje never saw the father of the cubs. Only once had he found the tracks of a big snow leopard, which he suspected could be the father.

Nono's world was his mother's home range - an area of about 30 square kilometres. She roamed the steep mountains with ridges, cliffs and rocky outcrops periodically patrolling and marking the boundaries of her **territory** with **fæces, scrapes** and urine. Snow leopards generally live in the high altitudes between 3,000 to 5,000 metres across the mountains of south and central Asia,

though in some cold and arid parts of Russia and Mongolia, they are sometimes found as low as 1,000 metres.

Dorje grew very fond of Nono. He even requested Hari to radio-collar the young leopard. Nono was about one-and-a-half years old and he could live on his own now. Hari thought about the idea, but decided against it. They had to monitor other radio-collared snow leopards and their prey. They could not take on more work at this time.

One day,

Dorje was tracking Dolma. After an hour of tough climbing, he found her tracks and those of the two female cubs, but there was no sign of Nono. For several days, he failed to find Nono's tracks. Had Nono left his mother? He was about two years old now, a time when male snow leopards separate from their mothers. Female cubs usually continue to live within their mother's home range or nearby, but males leave in search of their own territories.

Dorje stood outside his tent and searched the slopes for Nono everyday when he returned from work. He was sad and worried, but could not go on looking for Nono as he had to track Dolma. He silently prayed for the young leopard's well being.

# In Search of Nono

Three long anxious years had passed since Nono had gone missing. But, he was not the only one missing. Hari and his team had lost two of the four snow leopards they had radio-collared. One of them had managed to remove its radio-collar, as animals sometimes do! The other was Dolma – Nono's mother.

Dorje still remembered the day. It was a gloomy winter morning. The mountains and meadows were draped in a white sheet of knee-deep snow. The temperature was below freezing. Despite the bad weather, Dorje was tracking the collared leopards. He had struggled on the snow for a long time when he saw tracks. They looked about a day old. As he measured them, he knew they were Dolma's. Unfortunately, although Dolma still had the radio-collar around her neck, it had stopped working. The tracks were more closely spaced than normal. This meant that Dolma had been walking at a slow pace. He quickened his steps. Just as he was nearing a bend on the trail, he saw a grayish shape. "Dolma?" he wondered. She was lying on her side. Until then, Dorje had not suspected anything, but now there was a reason to. Dolma wasn't moving.

"How can she be lying motionless at this time of the day?" wondered Dorje. Why would such a secretive animal lie down in the open in broad daylight? Cautiously, he walked closer to the cat. When he was about 15 metres away, he threw a few snowballs in her direction to check if she moved. Should he go closer? He soon found himself standing next to Dolma's lifeless body, cold and dead. Tears rolling down his eyes, Dorje felt he had lost a dear friend. Someone so special and magnificent gone forever.

He went slowly back to the camp and gently broke the news to Hari. They reported the death to the Forest Department office at the nearest town, Kaza. A forest guard accompanied by a veterinary doctor came to the site a day later and conducted a **postmortem**. Dolma had died of old age and hunger; her stomach was completely empty. She was between nine and ten years old. Snow leopards in the wild seldom live beyond this age.

Back at the camp, the mood was sad and quiet. Hari and Dorje remembered the day they had radio-collared their first snow leopard. Dorje had followed her for nearly four years. She was the mother of his favourite snow leopard – *Nono*. Suddenly, a thought occurred to him. He turned to Hari and said, "Please let me look for Nono! We must find out where he is." This time, Hari agreed.

It did not take long for Dorje to spring into action. He had been waiting for this for a long time. He had already thought about which way Nono might have gone after leaving his mother. The most likely direction was towards the slopes above Kee which had two small villages - Gete and Tashigang. Dorje knew that there were two adult male snow leopards in this area, which was close to his own village of Kibber. He decided to explore Tashigang first, beginning the very next morning.

He got up early and left the village at dawn. A pair of binoculars hung from his neck. He also had a camera in his bag. He started walking towards the higher peaks and cliffs where he hoped to find some sign of Nono. He was unsure, yet hopeful that he would find his long-lost king.

After an hour's walk, he saw a herd of twelve bharal. They were busy **foraging**. It was an all-male herd. The larger animals had big horns that curved sideways forming a beautiful arch. The good naturalist he was, Dorje never trusted any observation to memory, no matter how small. He quickly noted the sighting down in his field diary and carried on. The path was steeper from here and he kept checking for snow leopard signs. A Himalayan **snowcock** was calling. Dorje knew this call well and had enjoyed hearing it from his childhood. As a teenager, he remembered going beyond his village with friends to look for

the bird's eggs, but this large and impressive **pheasant** was no longer as common as it used to be twenty years ago.

Further ahead, Dorje noticed footprints of a red fox – a small, common resident of the mountains. As he walked further, he noticed some movement on a steep slope above. It was a herd of ibex, a wild mountain goat much larger than the bharal, with massive curved horns. There were nine individuals in this herd. Over the years of working with Hari, Dorje had learnt to group these animals into different categoies according to their age and sex based on size, colour and the shape and size of their horns. He noted that there were five adult males with huge and impressive horns, three adult females, two young or sub-adult females, and two one year-olds also known as yearlings.

It was noon. Dorje decided to have his food and rest for a while. He was looking forward to reaching Tashigang soon. Sitting on a **lichen**-covered rock, he had a cold lunch. He then lay on his back to rest a bit. Before he knew it, he was fast asleep.

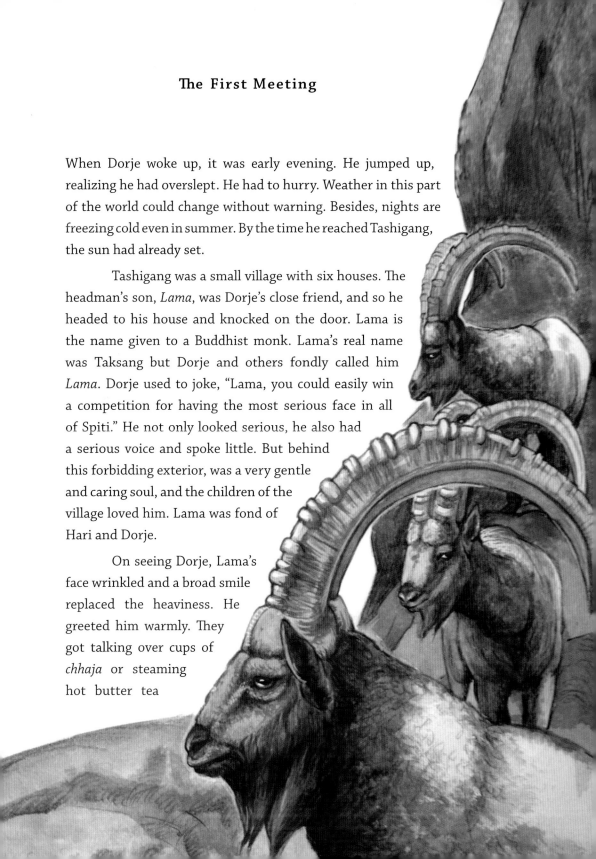

## The First Meeting

When Dorje woke up, it was early evening. He jumped up, realizing he had overslept. He had to hurry. Weather in this part of the world could change without warning. Besides, nights are freezing cold even in summer. By the time he reached Tashigang, the sun had already set.

Tashigang was a small village with six houses. The headman's son, *Lama*, was Dorje's close friend, and so he headed to his house and knocked on the door. Lama is the name given to a Buddhist monk. Lama's real name was Taksang but Dorje and others fondly called him *Lama*. Dorje used to joke, "Lama, you could easily win a competition for having the most serious face in all of Spiti." He not only looked serious, he also had a serious voice and spoke little. But behind this forbidding exterior, was a very gentle and caring soul, and the children of the village loved him. Lama was fond of Hari and Dorje.

On seeing Dorje, Lama's face wrinkled and a broad smile replaced the heaviness. He greeted him warmly. They got talking over cups of *chhaja* or steaming hot butter tea

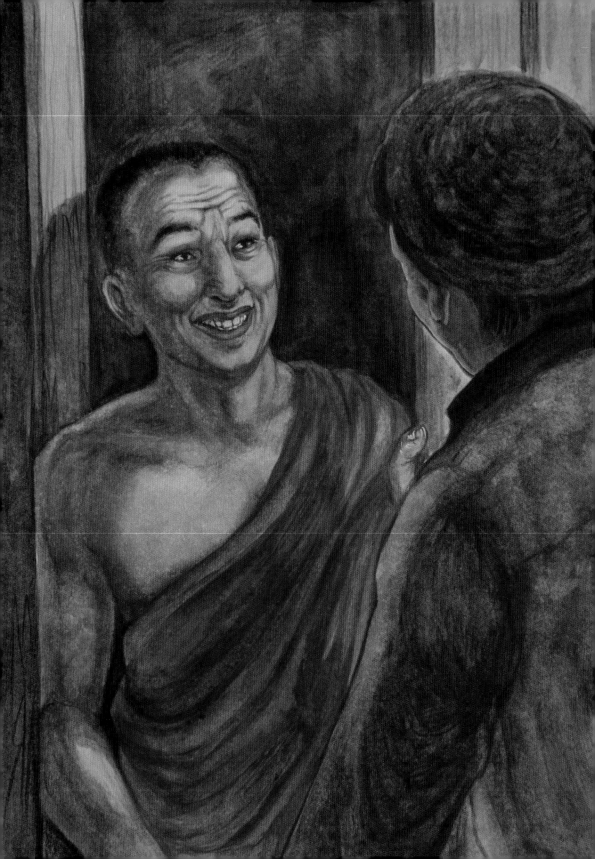

– a traditional salty brew that tasted more like soup than like tea.

"A yak calf was killed two days ago by a snow leopard. It is only partly eaten." Lama's words brought anticipation to Dorje's face. "Did anyone see the cat?" "No, but I saw its footprints, they were unmistakable," replied Lama. Dorje realized he had a good chance of seeing the animal. His heart was beating faster already! "I would like to go there to take a look tomorrow morning," he said. Lama smiled at his eagerness.

The next day dawned bright and sunny. Dorje went up to the terrace of Lama's house. From here, he could see the rooftops of houses all lined with thorny stacks of dried *Caragana*, contrasting with the whitewashed walls and brightly coloured red and blue windows and doors. The dried bushes were put in neat piles that looked pretty and also prevented the mud houses from getting damaged by the occasional summer rain. When Dorje came down, he saw Lama ready to leave with him. He was surprised. "Are you accompanying me?" Lama just smiled.

Both of them walked in silence towards the pasture where the yak calf had been killed. "You know Lama, Hari tells me that in Tibet and some parts of Ladakh, you still find wild yaks!" said Dorje. "Really? I have never seen any other than the domesticated ones we have here!" exclaimed Lama. "Yaks are amazing animals, aren't they? We use them for wool, meat, and to plough our fields. I sometimes wonder what we would do without them!" he added.

When they reached the site of the kill, the sun was overhead, but a few clouds had begun to gather. As they searched the slopes above, a grayish shape moved in the distance. It was a snow leopard, staring quizzically at them. "Look at the size of its head. It's a male," Dorje whispered. The snow leopard turned and disappeared into the snow, the way a magician would pull a cloak of invisibility around himself.

Just before the cat vanished, Dorje managed to see the twisted tail with his powerful binoculars. He now had one important clue that the snow leopard was indeed the cub that he had fondly named *Nono*. But he would have to wait before confirming this.

"I need to see his face," Dorje mumbled to himself. Just as they were about to move, a rustle caught their attention. A skulking red fox was trying to get closer to the kill to feed on it. It had probably lain hidden at some distance when the cat was on its kill. "Lucky fox! We have driven the leopard away and earned him an easy meal," said Lama. As they walked back towards Tashigang, Dorje was sure that the snow leopard would return to the kill. He also knew that some of the villagers could drive the

snow leopard away and take away the kill for
its meat. Worse still, a hunter could poison the
carcass. This was the surest way to kill a snow leopard,
and it happened occasionally. Not everyone was tolerant
of snow leopards. For many, the animal was just a pest that
occasionally killed their precious goats and yaks.

  The next day, Dorje decided to reach the kill site by
afternoon and watch over it from a distance. He left after
lunch and managed to reach the site within an hour. The kill
was not visible. Six big brownish shapes were huddled over
it. Himalayan Griffon Vultures – these birds had descended
on the kill and were feeding noisily on it. Their presence
indicated that the cat was not around. Dorje rested against
a rock and mused, "These vultures depend on snow
leopards and other **predators** to get their food. The
predators depend on bharal, ibex and other animals,
which depend on plants to survive. We too are a
part of this intricately woven web." Not for the
first time, Dorje was filled
with a renewed sense
of wonder at life

and all its mysteries. "So much to learn," thought Dorje as he settled into a more comfortable position, prepared to wait for a long time for the snow leopard to make his appearance.

Late in the evening the cat returned; earlier than Dorje had expected. This time Dorje managed to get a whole view of the animal through his binoculars. It was Nono! There was no mistaking that torn ear and twisted tail. Dorje was overjoyed, and couldn't wait to meet Hari and convince him to radio-collar Nono. Now was his chance to celebrate his reunion with the king.

# Belling the Cat!

It was the fifth winter of Nono's life. He was entering the peak of his adulthood.

Hari and Dorje were out in the snowclad mountains. Tashi and Sherpa trailed behind, dragging a reluctant goat with them. They had been on Nono's trail for a while. On reaching a suitable spot, Hari instructed them, "Put it up here. Get some boulders and rocks--it should look natural; don't forget that the predator is smart and will be suspicious of anything unusual." They were setting up a cage to trap Nono. By noon everything was in place. The hapless goat tied inside, probably sensing its fate, had started bleating loudly in protest. The trap was ready. If the snow leopard entered the cage to get the goat, the door would automatically shut.

Five days and nights went by without any success. One day, there were snow leopard tracks only a hundred metres away from the cage, but no sign closer than that. Nono was curious, but suspicious. Tashi and Sherpa complained about all the grass they had to carry to feed the goat every day. Hari and Dorje were taking it easy though. They had experienced this before, knowing it takes patience to catch a snow leopard. Lots of it!

Tashi and Sherpa had almost given up by now. Yet, on the sixth night, Nono, who had probably been hungry for several days, emerged from the darkness to inspect the bleating goat. Dorje, huddled inside his sleeping bag, was watching over the cage with his night-vision binoculars from a high rocky **outcrop**. Nono walked towards the cage, still a little suspicious. He took a long time sniffing and inspecting it and after deciding that it was safe enough, finally stepped in. As he entered, the door slammed shut. He tried to escape, but in vain. Angrily, he bit the bars. He roared as he threw himself against the cage, the fearsome sound shattering the silence of the Himalayan winter night.

It was three in the morning when Dorje informed Hari of their success. "We'll start the operation at daybreak; let us not take the risk of doing it at night. But, you keep a watch," Hari instructed. The first rays of dawn saw Hari and the team ready. Nono had put the goat out of its misery, but had not eaten it much. Hari held a **blowpipe** to his mouth, aimed at the trapped Nono. A powerful blast of air landed the **dart** with the **tranquilizing drug** precisely on Nono's thigh. Nono was startled on being hit and, after struggling for a while, fell into a deep slumber.

"This may appear easy and quick but one needs to be very careful while using the drug," Hari told Dorje and the others, as he examined Nono. "A high dose of the drug can kill the animal but if the dose is too low, then the animal won't go to sleep".

Lifting a tranquilized Nono out of the cage, Hari and Dorje quickly fitted a radio-collar around his neck. Tashi and Sherpa measured him and checked his physical condition. The entire operation was over in about forty-five minutes. Leaving Nono behind to recover, the team climbed up the rocky outcrop and watched. In an hour, Nono slowly awoke as the effect of the drug waned. He tried to stand up, and collapsed again, still drowsy from the **sedative**. This happened twice before he could finally move without trouble. As Nono walked away, Dorje watched him fade from sight. At last, he would be on Nono's trail in his own kingdom...he smiled at Hari happily.

Hari had to go back to Pin Valley to check on the collared snow leopards there. Dorje spent the next several months tracking Nono's movements by

himself. One morning, he decided to go to Kee to visit Sherpa. Dorje was tired of working alone and needed someone to help with his work. He found Sherpa repairing his mud house, which had begun leaking.

Kee was a picturesque village with a beautiful Buddhist monastery overlooking the Spiti valley. It was early June; late spring in the cold desert areas of the Himalaya. The herds of bharal were still in the lower altitudes, having descended at the onset of winter. Many Himalayan animals move to lower slopes where there is less snow and more grass to eat during winter, and return to the higher reaches as summer comes in. Their predator, the snow leopard, also follows.

As the morning rays hit the serene Kee monastery, Dorje knocked at Sherpa's door. His young son Lobsang, a boy with deep eyes and a bright smile, opened the door. "Apa, Dorje uncle is here!" Sherpa welcomed Dorje home, and over breakfast of tea and *tsampa* (roasted barley flour), Dorje explained the purpose of his visit. "I would like to leave tomorrow morning. Can you get someone to accompany me?" Sherpa nodded. "Why don't you take Namgyal with you? His knowledge of these mountains is very good. He is now in Tashigang."

Namgyal was a well-built man in his mid-twenties. He hailed from Gete. He had dropped out of school early and since then had roamed the mountains herding cattle, sheep and goats. His knowledge of the mountains and wildlife was immense, which is why Sherpa had suggested that Dorje take him along for assistance.

"Somehow, Sherpa, I'm not comfortable with Namgyal."

"Come on, now! I've inquired and they say he's very good . He is a herder, he is young and he loves the mountains. What else do you need, Dorje?"

"Sherpa, Hari insists that our men should not only like to work in the mountains, they must have the right conduct too."

"What do you mean by right conduct? What is wrong with him?"

"I have heard that Namgyal sometimes goes hunting. Can't you find anyone else, Sherpa?"

"Not really! You won't find anyone willing to slog day after day in the

mountains and at such short notice."

Sherpa continued, "If you can let me know by this afternoon, I can send word with any herder heading that way."

But Dorje replied firmly, "No, I will not take him this time."

"Alright! Alright! You always want the last word," snorted Sherpa.

"One thing more thing—I want to take Lobsang with me."

"Lobsang? Why, he is just a kid! What will he do there? Do you really think he can help you?" Sherpa was taken aback.

Around four in the afternoon, Sherpa shook a half-asleep Dorje and asked, "What have you decided?" "Lobsang comes with me," replied Dorje.

"All right. But, be careful. He is just a kid..." Sherpa turned to see Lobsang smiling at them.

Later at night, Dorje talked to the village elders about the state of the grazing pastures and the problems people were increasingly facing as snow leopards and wolves killed their yaks and other livestock.

Farming and rearing livestock are the chief occupations of people in this part of the Himalaya. Livestock provide milk, milk products and manure for fields. Fields in turn provide food and income. People use pastures (grazing lands) to graze their livestock herds. So, people and pastures are closely linked. If the pastures are healthy, livestock is healthy, which means prosperity for the people.

Dorje collected some important information from the villagers about cattle, goat and sheep

killed by snow leopards and wolves around Kee and noted it to share later with Hari.

Before going to bed, Dorje told Lobsang. "We'll leave early in the morning. And here, take this bag. Pack all your things neatly in it." It was a small rucksack; Lobsang was thrilled.

Early next morning, Dorje and Lobsang dragged themselves out of bed and stepped out. The sun had not yet risen and as they walked on the narrow path between the silent rows of houses, they could smell yak dung. The village was still asleep. At this time of the morning, the streets are normally the domain of the village dogs. Here, however, there were no dogs. The wolves made sure of that.

## On Nono's Trail

Dorje and Lobsang started climbing the mountain that rose above Kee. They carried enough food to last them a few days. In addition to the usual light waterproof tent and the radio-collar receiver control unit, Dorje's backpack included an extra sleeping bag. They reached their Tashigang camp in the afternoon.

After a simple meal, they headed for the slopes in Nono's home range. Dorje kept for a constant check for Nono's radio-collar signal until they reached a small rounded peak. It was an ideal place to camp. There were some rocks and a large hollow where they could take shelter if the winds picked up.

The altimeter read 4,600 metres. Despite the height, wildlife was still pretty abundant here. Many birds, including **buntings, larks, wheatears,** snowcocks and vultures, have made these mountains their home. The lynx, which is a wild cat, and pikas or mouse-hares, which are rat-sized relatives of hares also live in this cold, high and dry landscape.

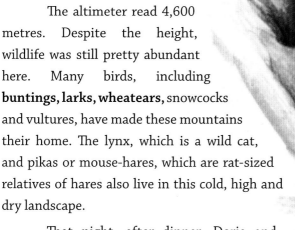

That night, after dinner, Dorje and Lobsang stretched out in their sleeping bags on a flat rock, facing the star-studded sky. It was a silvery moonlit night. In the stillness all around, they could hear a red fox on the move, nosing around for some food. The night was alive with activity, but Lobsang had quickly fallen into a deep sleep.

Suddenly a call pierced the calm of the night. Lobsang was startled, and asked in a soft tone, barely concealing his fear, "What was that sound?"

"Nothing to be afraid of, Lobsang," Dorje reassured him, "these are the calls of snow leopards– it is quite unusual to hear them, but when the male and female are together during the breeding season, they can create quite a racket!"

They heard it again. Louder now. Lobsang's fear turned to excitement. The calls were a strange combination of mewing and roaring, accompanied by the occasional growl or grunt.

Dorje remembered the antenna and fetched it. The signal was loud... *beep...beep...beep!* "It's Nono! He's found a partner! Hari will be delighted to hear this!" Dorje exclaimed.

Eventually, the calls grew faint. After a while, the night returned to its dark and silent ways.

# The Hidden Danger

The call of a snowcock was their morning wake-up alarm. Dorje imitated the call from inside his snug sleeping bag. The bird responded with an even louder call. This game continued for a while, much to Lobsang's delight.

Still in his sleeping bag, Dorje picked up the antenna and checked for a signal. There was none. Nono had moved. They had to move as well.

Nono and his mate had left neat pugmarks along the path. Assisted by Lobsang, Dorje carefully traced two pugmarks on thin sheets of paper. He chose the pugmarks on firm ground. "Too much snow or soft ground can distort the pugmark. These are perfect and give us a good idea of the size and identity of the animal."

They followed the tracks for about a kilometre. Dorje pointed out places where the cats had stopped or sat down. Combing the area closely, he collected a few snow leopard hairs from these spots. Lobsang was watching, eager to learn all that the older man could teach him. Dorje carefully placed the hairs in a plastic cover, and put it away in his backpack. "We can use them in a laboratory to identify individual snow leopards, and find out which of them are related to each other," he explained to a curious Lobsang. "You can ask Hari more about it when you meet."

After a kilometre the two sets of tracks diverged and the female's pugmarks disappeared. "Dorje uncle, there is only one set of tracks here!" pointed out Lobsang. "That's a good observation!" Dorje said, pleased. Lobsang beamed.

As they were walking, Dorje left the trail often to check for signals. Lobsang was enjoying the walk, and as it was daytime, he was unafraid. He wandered off the trail a few times to explore. At a bend, he climbed a large rock and peeped over it, and noticed a shiny object on the ground. He called out, "Dorje uncle, please come here!"

Just as Dorje reached him, Lobsang bent to pick up this strange new thing. "Lobsang! Don't touch it. You will get hurt!" The boy froze, fear all over his

face. Dorje reached him in two quick steps and knelt down. "It is a **snare**. Put here to catch wild animals."

He picked up a stick and pushed it into the trap. *Phut!* The snare clamped shut. The stick was 'caught'. Lobsang was horrified. "When a walking animal puts its foot in the snare, this is what happens. It is extremely painful and the animal suffers a lot. Slowly, it dies from pain and hunger," Dorje explained.

He looked worried. "What are you thinking about?" Lobsang asked, sensing the tension. "Someone here wants to trap innocent animals. Nono, too, could get caught," replied Dorje.

"Can't we take the snare away?"

"Certainly, we can do that, but then we'll never know who set it up. Besides, another will snare replace this one. Instead, let us spend the night nearby and wait to see if anyone comes to check on it. If nobody turns up, we'll remove it and move on."

They found themselves a hiding place among some boulders and squeezed into the narrow gaps between the rocks. Dorje kept vigil while Lobsang dozed on and off. Towards twilight, Dorje began to find it difficult to see clearly. His back, taking the brunt of his uncomfortable posture, was beginning to complain. He sat up and was about to rise when he noticed a figure approaching them from behind the boulders that concealed them. He woke Lobsang and they crouched quietly, hardly daring to breathe.

The stranger walked quietly and quickly past them, towards the snare. Checking for tracks, he suddenly looked up and around. "He has seen our footprints," Dorje whispered. "Why don't we catch him?" asked an impatient and tense Lobsang. "I'm waiting to see if he's alone. Otherwise we could be in trouble" Dorje replied.

The man looked around suspiciously. Dorje saw that he was not armed. He asked Lobsang to wait, and crept silently around the rocks, beyond where the stranger stood. Suddenly, almost like a predator, Dorje pounced on the man. Taken completely by surprise, Dorje's quarry barely moved. Before he could recover, Dorje caught him firmly, twisted his arm and knocked him to the ground.

The man fell.

In the fading light Dorje saw his face. He could hardly believe his eyes. "Namgyal?!" The man was in for a shock too. "Dorje?!" he mumbled. Dorje shook him by the collar shouting, "How long have you been doing this?"

Still hiding, Lobsang watched the drama unfold.

It was a while before Namgyal spoke. "Let go of me! Why do you care what I do?" asked Namgyal angrily. "Let me do my work, you do yours!"

"You are killing innocent animals! We study snow leopards to protect them, but you put out snares to trap them!" Dorje continued calmly now, "And don't forget - you are also breaking our traditional Buddhist rules by hunting."

"Do you think I do this for pleasure? What happens when *your* snow leopards kill our livestock? What do you have to say about that?" Namgyal retorted in a loud and angry voice.

"A snow leopard cannot eat grass! It has to kill animals to survive," Dorje was gentle but maintained a sharp gaze at Namgyal.

"Yes, but there are bharal and ibex and so many other animals for them to eat. Livestock are our livelihood," Namgyal was quieter now, realizing that Dorje would not harm him.

Namgyal sat down. It was now nearly dark. Lobsang emerged from behind the boulders. Namgyal shone his torch. "It's Lobsang, Sherpa's son," Dorje told him.

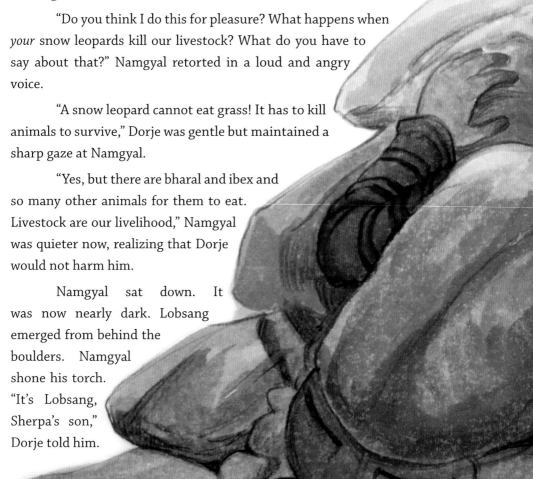

"I did not take to hunting and trapping without reason. First it was anger at the wolves and snow leopards that killed our livestock and later it was for the meat of bharal and other animals."

Dorje put his hand on Namgyal's shoulder.

"I know, Namgyal. Remember, I am one of you, and understand what you must be going through. But there are so few ibex and bharal left right now because *we* have taken most of the pastures for our livestock. You must understand that snow leopards need animals like the bharal and ibex to survive. If wild animals are few and livestock many, it is obvious that they will kill domestic animals. They are also easier to catch," Dorje tried to reason with him.

"You may think about the snow leopard's survival, but people don't. We have to think about *our own* survival," Namgyal responded.

"I too have lost animals to snow leopards and wolves," said Dorje.

"We can't blame wild animals for all our misery. Have you forgotten what Lord Buddha has taught us? To respect life, be it a snow leopard or a human being."

Namgyal remained quiet.

"How many snow leopards have you snared? And who are you doing this for?" Dorje's voice grew a bit louder.

"None at all. I've killed a wolf and some bharal though. I have shared the bharal meat with others in my village," Namgyal replied without hesitation.

He sounded honest and for the first time, Dorje saw a ray of hope.

"Is there anyone else involved in this?" Dorje was now grilling him.

"Absolutely not, why do you ask?"

"Don't you know that you can be punished for this crime? It is illegal to kill the wild animals you are snaring. Shall I hand you over to Mr. Sharma, at Kaza?" Namgyal realized that Dorje was now talking tough. He would be in trouble if Dorje reported him to the Forest Department.

He pleaded, "I have children."

"Other people have children too, but they don't take to hunting to make a living," Dorje looked him in the eye and spoke quietly.

Namgyal was silent for a while. Then he looked up and asked, "But we have to do something to save our livestock from being killed by snow leopards, don't we?"

"Perhaps we can be more careful when we herd the livestock and not let them stray too far. That way we could prevent some of the deaths. Look, I know it is difficult, and I don't have all the answers. But I am sure that the solution is not in killing these beautiful animals. We must remember that they also have a right to this place. This is as much *their* home as ours."

The moon had risen and their faces were faintly visible.

"I am giving you a chance now, but if you are seen again in this area; I will hand you over to…"

"No! Dorje, please don't do that! I will stay away."

"Go now. And leave this snare here." Dorje sent him off with a warning look.

Everything was quiet again.

It was close to midnight. Dorje lit a fire and cooked them a simple meal. Lobsang was very quiet. He had never seen Dorje so furious, and was a little afraid of him. To ease his fears, Dorje told him funny stories about his boyhood, which made Lobsang laugh until his stomach hurt. Still giggling, the young boy fell asleep by the fire.

# The Hunt

Morning brought another beautiful and clear day. When Dorje awoke, Lobsang was still fast asleep. Yellow-billed choughs – the crows of the high altitudes – were already flying around. Their raucous calls finally woke Lobsang up.

Dorje went to fetch water leaving Lobsang to take care of their belongings. Lying on his stomach, Lobsang watched the choughs performing mid-air acrobatics. They looked as if they were having a competition for the most agile bird.

A voice spoke up behind him, "*Julley*, little boy!" Namgyal was standing near the remains of the fire.

"Did you not go home?" asked a surprised Lobsang.

"No, I spent the night in a cave nearby," replied Namgyal. "Where is Dorje?"

"He'll be here soon...there he is!"

Dorje was surprised and a little angry. "What are you doing here? You should have been back at the village!"

Namgyal didn't look up. Hesitantly, he replied, "I have been thinking about what you said yesterday, all through the night. I wanted to apologise...and to explain about snare... please understand...I was in urgent need of money, that's why I laid that snare."

Namgyal shifted uneasily from foot to foot as he spoke to Dorje.

Dorje knew this was difficult for Namgyal, but he had to be sure that the words were sincere. He let Namgyal continue.

Looking straight into Dorje's eyes, Namgyal pleaded, "Please give me a chance. I...I would like to work with you...do you think I could?"

"And earn some honest money, eh?" Dorje sounded kinder.

Namgyal nodded.

"Hmm. I suppose you can join us, but I won't pay you anything until Hari agrees," Dorje relented.

Dorje was still somewhat unsure about taking Namgyal along but, deep down, he knew that Namgyal was a good sort.

Silently, he said a prayer for their safe journey.

The day's agenda was to continue looking for wild animals, along the way to their final destination, *Tsankar*. This was a vast pasture where villagers grazed their sheep, goats and cattle.

At regular intervals, Dorje stopped to scan the slopes around for wildlife. It was nearly noon when he spotted a herd of bharal on the slope opposite the one they were on. He counted forty-six animals. It was a mixed herd with adult males and females and younger animals as well. As the animals were too far way to see well through the binoculars, Dorje set up the **spotting scope** for Namgyal and Lobsang.

"Try counting the animals," he told Namgyal.

"How difficult can that be?" thought Namgyal. Yet after ten minutes of being glued to the scope he swung around with a look of frustration. "This is terribly difficult. It requires more patience than trapping! Darn! I've lost count three times! Let me start again!"

Dorje laughed, warming up slightly to Namgyal.

They resumed walking after Dorje had taken notes. A little ahead, Dorje stopped and showed Lobsang a tiny plant. "Smell it," he said. To his surprise, Lobsang found the plant had a nice, strong smell of spice. "What is this?" he asked. "It's called **thyme**. In some countries, people use it to flavour food," Dorje told them.

As they were talking, some movement on the ground some distance away caught Dorje's attention. "Look!" he pointed. "Tibetan Sandgrouse. They feed mainly on seeds of grass and other plants. Here, take a look through this," Dorje

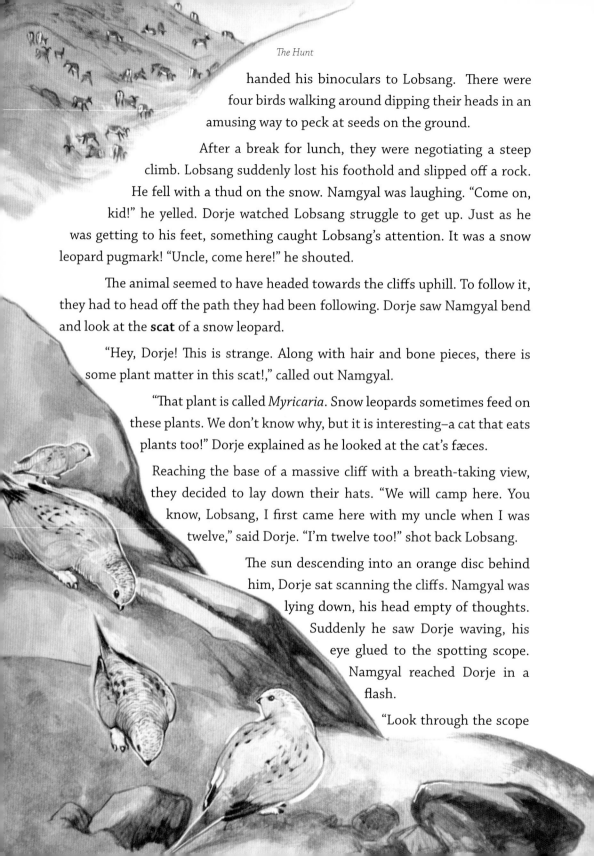

handed his binoculars to Lobsang. There were four birds walking around dipping their heads in an amusing way to peck at seeds on the ground.

After a break for lunch, they were negotiating a steep climb. Lobsang suddenly lost his foothold and slipped off a rock. He fell with a thud on the snow. Namgyal was laughing. "Come on, kid!" he yelled. Dorje watched Lobsang struggle to get up. Just as he was getting to his feet, something caught Lobsang's attention. It was a snow leopard pugmark! "Uncle, come here!" he shouted.

The animal seemed to have headed towards the cliffs uphill. To follow it, they had to head off the path they had been following. Dorje saw Namgyal bend and look at the **scat** of a snow leopard.

"Hey, Dorje! This is strange. Along with hair and bone pieces, there is some plant matter in this scat!," called out Namgyal.

"That plant is called *Myricaria*. Snow leopards sometimes feed on these plants. We don't know why, but it is interesting–a cat that eats plants too!" Dorje explained as he looked at the cat's fæces.

Reaching the base of a massive cliff with a breath-taking view, they decided to lay down their hats. "We will camp here. You know, Lobsang, I first came here with my uncle when I was twelve," said Dorje. "I'm twelve too!" shot back Lobsang.

The sun descending into an orange disc behind him, Dorje sat scanning the cliffs. Namgyal was lying down, his head empty of thoughts. Suddenly he saw Dorje waving, his eye glued to the spotting scope. Namgyal reached Dorje in a flash.

"Look through the scope

exactly where I tell you to," commanded Dorje.

"Do you see that large cliff? Below that is a sharp slope. To the left of that you will see three large boulders."

"Yes..."

"Focus your gaze on the boulder to the right and look for movement."

"Oh, yes – the ghost of the snow!" Namgyal said softly.

Dorje said, "Call the boy. Where is he?"

Namgyal discovered Lobsang gathering dry *Caragana* brushes to make a fire. He told him about the snow leopard. Dropping his armload, Lobsang was by Dorje's side in a moment.

He looked through Dorje's spotting scope, but couldn't see anything except rocks. "But where? I just can't see any animal there."

"Be patient and look carefully among the boulders."

Suddenly, the cat moved. "There! I can see it now!"

Dorje nodded and lowered his voice. "Can you see the radio-collar around its neck?" "Yes. It's our Nono!" came the excited reply.

Nono was crouching on the ground and slowly inching towards a herd of foraging bharal. He was **camouflaged** in the boulders above them. Some bharal were moving up unaware that Nono was waiting in ambush. Still     crouching, he moved closer to a young male animal.

"Can't the bharal see or smell him?" asked Lobsang in a low voice.

"Shhh! Just watch now. I will answer you later."

As Lobsang watched Nono creeping forward he realized how well the animal's body was designed for the terrain. His flattened snout and dull coat blotched with brown and white concealed him completely against the grey-brown rocky background. The long, thick tail gave him balance in this steep place. Padded feet made no sound, letting Nono approach his quarry noiselessly. He was so close to the bharal, they could probably have heard him breathe! They seemed to notice nothing, and continued to forage. Nono pressed himself close to the rock, and seemed to just vanish into it.

Five minutes passed since Nono had vanished among the rocks. Then, without warning, the rocks came to life, and Nono burst into the herd of bharal, his paws spread out, and his mouth in a snarl.

It was over in an instant. The rest of the bharal herd fled. Nono emerged with a single male bharal in his jaws. The doomed animal struggled briefly, his hind legs trembling violently, but soon     gave up. Nono did not let go of the bharal's neck for a long time, and                 only after he was certain the animal was dead did he                 loosen his grip. Slowly, he laboured up and disappeared                 into the cliffs with his hard-earned meal.

# The New Camp

Exhasuted by a tough day's walk, Dorje, Namgyal and Lobsang reached *Tsankar*. A huge expanse of excellent foraging pasture for wild herbivores and livestock, it belonged to Dorje's village Kibber. Dorje had earlier suggested to Hari that they could encourage the village council to stop livestock grazing in some parts of this tract, and set it aside entirely for wild animals.

The camp set up and all in order, the three ventured out to find a nice place to sit and enjoy the view. A large bird glided in ever-widening circles overhead. "You see that bird? It is a vulture called Lammergeier. It feeds on meat and bone marrow, which it gets by dropping the bones on rocks and breaking them open." Dorje never lost a chance to introduce Lobsang to a new animal, bird or plant. He was a good teacher, particularly when he was talking about wildlife, and he had keen pupils in Lobsang and Namgyal.

Earlier, while organizing the camp, Lobsang had pointed to a plant with large, spinach-like leaves and said, "I think it is the plant which stores water. Once when I was out in the fields with my father there was no water to drink, and he had given me its leaf-stalk to chew. It quenched my thirst." "You're right!" Dorje had been impressed. "The plant is called **Rheum**. It should be used only in an emergency as your father did."

They also spotted a few more herds of bharal. "If we can protect some of the pastures from livestock, Hari says we would have herds of up to hundred bharal." "Hundred bharal?! That would be quite a sight. But, Dorje, what would the livestock eat then?" Namgyal expressed his surprise and concern.

Dorje laughed and said, "I

don't mean that we should give up our land altogether! I'm only talking about protecting small parts of our grazing grounds for wild animals. There would still be plenty for our livestock." "Hmmm...I suppose that is possible," mused Namgyal.

They spent three days at this camp walking different trails and observing wildlife. Nono was around – they managed to pick up his signal on all three days, but never saw him.

The five days outdoors transported Lobsang to another world. He once asked Dorje, "Why don't they teach us about these things at school?"

"What 'things'?"

"About the creatures that live around us and about things that can affect us, like a storm or snowfall. I would enjoy it so much more than the geography my textbook contains!"

"And it would be useful too," Dorje added.

The team had just finished with another day's work. They were walking leisurely back to camp, when Namgyal asked, "Dorje, do you think I can join this project and work with you full time?" Dorje said nothing. Namgyal was in talkative mood. The past few days had taught him a lot about himself. "I am tired of a life of hunting and trapping. But, earlier I did not think there was a choice. I don't own land to till and have too few livestock to earn a living from. I have lost most of them to wolves and snow leopards."

"That is the problem Hari and all of us are trying to find solutions to. He plans to help us start an insurance programme, which will provide us protection against livestock losses to snow leopards and wolves. If this works well, we might see a totally changed picture in Spiti." Dorje sounded positive.

"Getting back to work – as I told you earlier, we shall begin your training once Hari agrees. In the mean time, you help me with tracking Nono. Sherpa and Lama will arrive with supplies tomorrow and take Lobsang back with them."

Namgyal only nodded.

Next day, loaded with fresh supplies brought in by Lama and Sherpa, Dorje said goodbye to his young friend. Namgyal stayed back with him. Through Sherpa, he also sent news to Hari about Namgyal's request to join and about everything else that had taken place.

# First Lessons

At the end of the plateau where *Tsankar* was located, the valley sloped into a narrow gorge and rose steeply to culminate in a series of cliffs. A mosaic of snow, vegetation and bare rocks lay ahead. To the casual onlooker, it appeared barren and devoid of life. The animals merged so well with their surroundings, it required a skilled person to spot them. Here, each rock, each patch of vegetation was a potential site to look for resting bharal or other animals.

Namgyal was excellent at spotting and tracking animals. But, he needed to learn more than that: collecting information systematically and organizing it. So, training was essential. "This is how you must hold the antenna. This box is for setting the frequency. By moving this knob to number four, you will receive a signal from Nono's collar if he is within the range of this antenna," Dorje explained.

"When we receive a signal or sight an animal, we record it – like this." Dorje taught him how the data sheets were used. He also took out his field diary and showed Namgyal the kind of information he had recorded. Namgyal listened in silence, asking questions only when he had a doubt. He was a confident man made for the mountains.

As they walked they chatted about the plants and animals along the way. Namgyal knew most of the local names, and Dorje told him the English and scientific names that he had learnt from Hari. *Caragana. Stipa. Alium. Rosa.*

They neared a cliff. From the edge, it was possible to view a large area. With his binoculars, Dorje scanned the slopes. He could spot three different herds of bharal. He passed the binoculars to Namgyal and asked him to try. "See if you can spot any bharal or ibex." Namgyal spotted the three herds. After a while, he pointed to the west. "Ibex!"

Binoculars to his eyes, Dorje scanned the area. "You are right Namgyal, there are three ibex. All are males in class IV."

"Now, what is *that*?" Namgyal laughed. "I didn't know ibex went to school!" he said with a mischievous look.

Dorje laughed too, and then explained, "Male ibex can be separated into groups or classes based on the size of their horns. The older an ibex is, the larger and more impressive his horns become."

He pointed to one of the males and said, "Look there, the male on left has horns that go high and diverge to go down in an arch. It's a class IV male. The males of different age classes are often found together."

"And why are we so interested in ibex?" asked Namgyal, "Aren't we here to study Nono?"

"Yes," explained Dorje patiently, "but in order to understand the snow leopard, we have to understand what it eats. Ibex form an important part of a snow leopard's **diet**. Here ibex are not very common as compared to bharal, but in Pin Valley there are no bharal at all, so snow leopards there depend mostly on ibex for food." Namgyal was visibly surprised. His head was buzzing with questions. He had been in these mountains so long, yet he felt he was beginning to find out about them all over again.

Walking beside him, Dorje was happy because Namgyal was interested and appeared to be learning quickly. In this terrain and testing weather, one doesn't just need tough people, one also needs men with keen eyes and sharp minds.

As the two men walked leisurely, a stone marten ran across the path and disappeared behind lichen-clad boulders some distance away. "There goes a naughty animal! There is a particular one that often enters my house to steal meat," said Namgyal.

A flock of small birds flew overhead, wings beating rapidly, quickly vanishing from sight. "Finches," pointed Dorje, "they have returned from their winter **migration**." Namgyal was surprised when Dorje told him that rosefinches often live in pastures above 5,000 metres.

"As a kid I used to go up the mountains beyond my village. Once I stumbled upon some eggs in a small scrape between rocks. They looked just like chicken eggs, but had a reddish tinge. My friend thought someone must have

hidden them and was going to collect them, but I stopped him. Later, I learnt that they were eggs of Himalayan snowcock." Dorje added with a chuckle, "So, you did believe in protecting wildlife at some point in your life!" Despite himself, Namgyal had to smile at Dorje's gentle teasing.

Several weeks went by. One day, a passing herder brought a message. "Hari sir is happy to hire Namgyal as an assistant." Dorje broke the news to Namgyal, watching his expression. He continued, "I've noticed that he always gives anyone who wants to help save wildlife a chance. You are a part of our team from this moment!" He also added that Hari had said that Namgyal would have to prove himself to become a permamnet member of research crew.

Namgyal had no words to respond with. In a choked voice he said, "Thank you. I will not disappoint you." Evening had descended on the mountains bringing a new dawn into Namgyal's life.

# The Last Journey

It was the month of February – peak winter in Spiti. Nono was now eight years old. It was exactly three years since he had been radio-collared, but the collar was no longer functional. So, Dorje had been tracking Nono and other snow leopards mainly through their pugmarks and kills reported by herders and village folk. Namgyal was a permanent and integral member of the snow leopard research team. He had attained a new perspective on life and had begun enjoying himself.

One morning, Namgyal heard from a fellow villager that a snow leopard had got caught in a snare. Dorje and he dropped everything they were doing and nearly ran all the way to the spot. Even as they approached the slain snow leopard, Dorje felt a sense of coldness sweep over him. Kneeling beside the great cat, all his fears were realised.

Nono was dead.

Stilled by pain and sorrow, Dorje could do nothing but stare at Nono's calm, empty face. Namgyal stood motionless beside him. He slowly put his hand on Dorje's back and sat down. The two men said nothing. Nono had probably struggled in the trap for at least three days before the wounds and hunger brought his life to an end. One more snow leopard had succumbed to human cruelty. If things continued this way much longer, this unique predator could soon go extinct.

They lifted Nono's body to take back it to the camp. Just as Dorje was about to move, he noticed a set of leopard tracks leading away. The tracks were of a female snow leopard. He turned to Namgyal and said in an urgent voice, "Please follow the tracks and find out where they lead."

Namgyal wept silently as he walked away. The animal that had changed his destiny was no more. His pain was all the deeper as he knew from personal experience what motivated the hunter who had set the trap. He realised with a pang that if circumstances had not changed, the snare that had killed Nono could

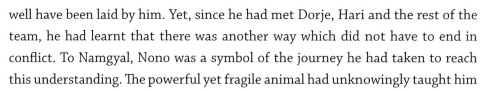

well have been laid by him. Yet, since he had met Dorje, Hari and the rest of the team, he had learnt that there was another way which did not have to end in conflict. To Namgyal, Nono was a symbol of the journey he had taken to reach this understanding. The powerful yet fragile animal had unknowingly taught him so much about the mountains that were his home. Namgyal made an inward resolution that Nono would not have died in vain, that the snow leopard's legacy would live on in the mountains.

Through these somber times, there was one note of cheer. Namgyal had followed the pugmarks that led away from Nono's corpse. What he had found filled everyone at the camp with new hope. "The tracks led to a cave", said Namgyal, "I saw pugmarks leading inside."

All of them had the same thought: "The female snow leopard we saw with Nono is going to have cubs! The king will return after all…"

Nono was buried in *Tsankar*. A life that had given joy and purpose to so many, had gone before its time. Lobsang learned about Nono's death later from Sherpa. Nono had been his first snow leopard – his special friend.

Nono's death was a big blow for Hari and his team. Years of effort had met with such a sudden and sad end. That year, they launched the livestock insurance programme in

Kibber. They also convinced the village council to set up the first 'village wildlife reserve' by stopping livestock grazing in *Tsankar*.

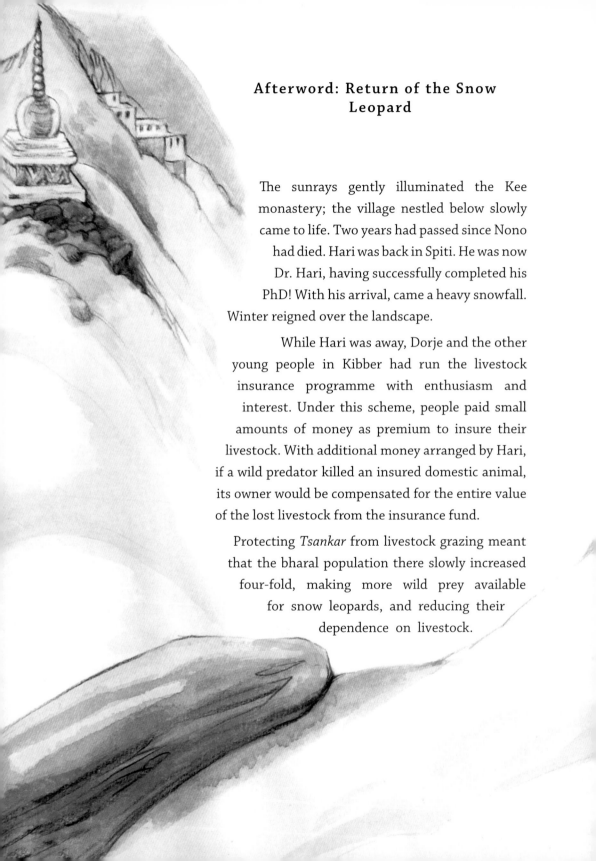

# Afterword: Return of the Snow Leopard

The sunrays gently illuminated the Kee monastery; the village nestled below slowly came to life. Two years had passed since Nono had died. Hari was back in Spiti. He was now Dr. Hari, having successfully completed his PhD! With his arrival, came a heavy snowfall. Winter reigned over the landscape.

While Hari was away, Dorje and the other young people in Kibber had run the livestock insurance programme with enthusiasm and interest. Under this scheme, people paid small amounts of money as premium to insure their livestock. With additional money arranged by Hari, if a wild predator killed an insured domestic animal, its owner would be compensated for the entire value of the lost livestock from the insurance fund.

Protecting *Tsankar* from livestock grazing meant that the bharal population there slowly increased four-fold, making more wild prey available for snow leopards, and reducing their dependence on livestock.

People were not only becoming more tolerant of snow leopards, they were beginning to see themselves as responsible custodians of the wildlife with which they shared their lands.

While he was away, Hari too had worked hard to garner more support for this programme. Some people he had talked to were convinced and ready to fund his scheme while a few were less sure. But Hari kept up the effort.

"Dorje, I have managed to get some money to expand the livestock insurance programme. If all the four villages around Kibber get involved, we can reduce the conflict between people and snow leopards. This way, we'll set an example of co-existence between people and wildlife in all of Spiti."

Dorje was happy to hear this. He worked hard to constitute livestock insurance committees in the villages and the insurance programme was expanded.

Today, the insurance programme is in its fifth year. No snow leopard or wolf has been killed in or around the five villages during this time. People are extremely happy and satisfied with the scheme. Dorje, Namgyal, Tashi, Sherpa and many other young people run the scheme in their own villages. Lama travels between villages, reading scriptures and preaching, amongst other things, the importance of protecting wildlife. Several tourists now accompany the 'snow leopard men' of Spiti to learn more about the Himalaya and to experience the joy of the mountains.

And Lobsang is the youngest researcher in the snow leopard project now! He is eighteen and spends most of his time observing wildlife. He has seen snow leopards on a few more occasions and is a happy young man. He is involved in conserving what he cared for from his childhood - *his* mountain environment.

And yes, recently he has sighted two snow leopards in the *Tsankar* pasture; an adult female and a grown male cub. Based on the tracks and sightings, he has discovered it is the same female who was with Nono when he was snared. This means the cub accompanying her is Nono's son...a new king is on the prowl!

Hari and Dorje's dream is slowly taking shape...the snow leopard has returned.

# Glossary

**Altimeter -** An instrument used to measure the altitude of a place or an object above a defined level. Usually we measure altitude of a place from sea level.

**Blowpipe –** A hunting tool consisting of a small tube one end of which has a place for a dart. The hunter/user blows into the other end, forcing the dart out. Hunters often tip the dart with poison. They are used primarily to hunt small animals such as monkeys. Scientists often use blowpipes with darts tipped with tranquilizers to **sedate** trapped wild animals to radio-collar them.

**Buntings -** A group of birds resembling the finches. They have strong, conical beaks and feed on seeds.

**Camouflage –** A way of concealing oneself, usually through an appearance that merges with the surroundings. Many animals and birds are coloured such that they cannot be seen easily by their predators or prey.

*Caragana* **-** A group of flowering plants found in Asia and Europe. The species found in Spiti looks like a spiky cushion. Local people use it as a fuel, protective material on terraces against rain, and as decoration.

**Carcass -** Dead body, usually referring to an animal.

**Dart -** A tranquilizer dart is a small, sharp object that has been tipped with a sedative. When the dart hits the wild animal, it causes the animal to fall into a deep sleep.

**Diet –** The food and drink ordinarily consumed by a person or animal.

**Fæces –** Waste matter passed out through the anus.

**Foraging –** Searching for food, handling it and eating it. Usually foraging is used to desbribe the way wild animals look for food.

**Habitat -** The natural environment of an organism, the place that is natural for the life and growth of an organism.

**Home range -** Area traversed by an animal for food gathering, mating, and caring for young. In practical terms, home range of wild animals refers to an estimate of the area used by the animal in m$^2$ or km$^2$ units.

**Larks** – Larks are small ground-dwelling birds which often sing beautiful songs. These birds nest on the ground and like several other ground birds, have long hind claws and are fairly dull in appearance. Larks feed on insects and seeds.

**Lichen** – A complex, often greenish or brown-grey crust-like organism that grows on rocks and trees. It is a mutually helpful coexistance of two groups of microorganisms - fungii and algae.

**Migration** - To go periodically from one region or climate to another, as certain birds, fishes, and animals do. Often they go from harsh climates to more pleasant weather, and return after the difficult season has passed.

**Outcrop** – A raised, flat area of land. Usually used to describe such places in the mountains.

**Postmortem** – Also known as autopsy, it is a medical procedure of examining dead bodies to find out what caused the animal or person to die. It is usually performed by a specialized medical doctor.

**Pheasants** - A group of large birds which are found in many parts of the world and are hunted for their meat. The peacock is a bird of the pheasant family, as is the common chicken. Among pheasants, there are clear differences between the appearance and size of males and females. Male pheasants are brightly coloured and usually possess crests, wattles and trains (long tails). They are usually larger than the females.

**Predator** – An animal that 'preys on' or catches and eats other animals.

**Prey** - An animal hunted or seized for food, especially by a carnivorous animal.

**Pugmarks** – Footprints of large predatory mammals such as tigers, lions, leopards and snow leopards. Spur, tracks and footprints are general terms that are used for all animals.

**Radio-collar** - A strap applied on the neck of an animal and fitted with a transmitter, an electric device which emits a signal. This signal can be received by an antenna. Scientists use radio-collaring to study species such as the snow leopard which are elusive, nocturnal or rare.

**Rheum –** Commonly known as Rhubarb, these are herbs with large, somewhat triangular leaves on long, fleshy stalks. Found only in Asia, they have long been used in traditional Chinese medicine, and more recently as food.

**Scat –** A specific term for excreta (stools) of carnivorous animals such as members of cat and dog families. Droppings and fæces are the terms used for excreta of wild animals in general.

**Scrape –** A mark used to announce the territory, generally made by a predatory animal (such as a cat or a dog) by scratching the ground with its claws. A snow leopard's scrape is a roundish or oval depression compared to that of a common leopard which generally makes a long and narrow scrape. Cats sometimes urinate or defecate in their scrapes.

**Sedative -** A drug/medicine that makes you go into a deep sleep. See **tranquilizing drug** below.

**Snare -** One of the simplest and most effective traps for hunting wild animals, made of wire, rope or metal. A snare works like the leash for a dog, and as the animal struggles, the snare tightens and chokes it.

**Snowcocks -** A group of birds of the **pheasant** family found in the montains of Eurasia including the Himalaya. In India, two species – the Himalayan snowcock and the Tibetan snowcock are found. Snowcocks are ground-nesting birds feeding on plants, their seeds and insects. Snow leopards and other carnivores of the Himalaya sometimes prey on snowcocks.

**Spotting scope –** An instrument more powerful than binoculars, used for viewing objects that are far away. Usually it has a single eyepiece, and is set up using a stand.

**Territory –** The area that an animal uses to find food, etc., and defends against other animals, especially of the same species.

**Thyme –** A large group of herbs form the Thyme family. Different species of thyme or *Thymus* have been commonly used in cooking and for their nectar. The ancient Greeks used it as fragrance in baths and as incense, even thinking that thyme was a source of courage!

**Tranquilizing drugs/tranquilizers –** Also known as sedatives, these are drugs or medicines that slow down some functions of your body, and make you calm, sleepy, slow your breathing, etc. They are used to sedate animals when they are radio-collared.

**Wheatears –** These are ground-dwelling, insect-eating birds of open and dry terrain. They often nest in spaces between rocks or disused burrows. Males are more colourful than females as in the case of most birds.